Raggedy Ann & Andy

A Read-Aloud Treasury

By Johnny Gruelle

Contents

How Raggedy Ann and Andy Came to Marcella's House

arcella liked to play up in the attic at Grandma's quaint old house way out in the country, for there were so many old forgotten things to find up there.

One day when Marcella was up in the attic and had played with the old spinning wheel until she had grown tired of it, she curled up on an old horsehair sofa to rest.

I wonder what is in that barrel, back in the corner? she thought, as she jumped from the sofa and climbed over two dusty trunks to the barrel standing back under the eaves.

It was quite dark back there, so when Marcella had pulled a large bundle of things from the barrel, she took them over to the window where she could see better. There was a funny little bonnet with long white ribbons. Marcella put it on.

In an old bag she found a number of old photographs of odd-looking men and women in old-fashioned clothes. And there was one picture of a very pretty little girl with long curls tied tightly back from her forehead and wearing a long dress and white pantaloons that reached to her shoe-tops. And then out of the heap she pulled an old rag doll with only one shoe-button eye, a painted nose, and a smiling mouth. Her dress was of soft material, blue with pretty little flowers and dots all over it.

Forgetting everything else in the happiness of her find, Marcella snatched up the rag doll and ran downstairs to show it to Grandma.

"Well! Well! Where did you find it?" Grandma cried. "It's old Raggedy Ann!" She hugged the doll to her chest. "I had forgotten her."

"She has been in the attic for fifty years, I guess!" said Grandma. "Well! Well! Dear old Raggedy Ann! I will sew another button on her right away!" Grandma went to the sewing-machine drawer and took out her needle and thread.

Marcella watched the sewing while Grandma explained how she had played with Raggedy Ann when she was a little girl.

"Now!" Grandma said when she was finished. "Raggedy Ann, you have two fine shoe-button eyes, and with them you can see the changes that have taken place in the world while you have been shut up so long in the attic! For, Raggedy Ann, you have a new playmate and mistress now, and I hope you both will have as much happiness together as you and I used to have!"

Then Grandma gave Raggedy Ann to Marcella, saying very seriously, "Marcella, let me introduce my very dear friend, Raggedy Ann. Raggedy, this is my granddaughter, Marcella!" And Grandma gave the doll a twitch with her fingers in such a way that the rag doll nodded her head to Marcella.

"Oh, Grandma! Thank you ever and ever so much!" Marcella cried as she gave Grandma a hug and kiss. "Raggedy Ann and I will have loads of fun."

And this is how Raggedy Ann joined the doll family at Marcella's house. Soon Raggedy Ann was a much beloved member of the doll family, which included the French doll, poor Susan (who had fallen and cracked her head), Henny the Dutch doll, Uncle Clem, the tin soldier, the Jumping Jack, and more.

Then one day Daddy took Raggedy Ann down to his office and propped her up against some books upon his desk; he wanted to see her cheery smile all day, for as you must surely know, smiles and happiness are truly catching.

Daddy wished to catch a whole lot of Raggedy Ann's cheeriness and happiness and to put it all down on paper so that those who did not have Raggedy Ann dolls might see just how happy and smiling a rag doll can be.

So Raggedy Ann stayed in Daddy's studio for three or four days.

She was missed very, very much at home and Marcella really longed for her, but she knew that Daddy was borrowing some of Raggedy Ann's sunshine, so she did not complain.

Raggedy Ann did not complain either, for no one (not even a rag doll) ever complains if they have such happiness about them.

One evening, just as Daddy was finishing his day's work, a messenger boy came with a package—a nice, soft lumpy package.

Daddy opened the nice, soft lumpy package and found a letter.

Grandma had told Daddy, long before this, that at the time Raggedy Ann was made, a neighbor lady had made a boy doll, Raggedy Andy, for her little girl, who always played with Grandma.

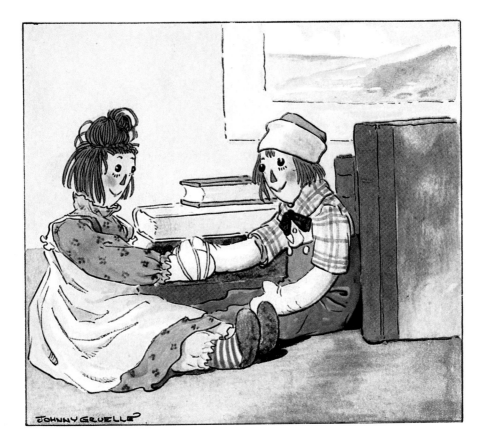

And when Grandma told Daddy this, she wondered whatever had become of her little playmate and the boy doll, Raggedy Andy.

After reading the letter, Daddy opened the other package, which had been inside the nice, soft lumpy package and found—Raggedy Andy.

Raggedy Andy's soft floppy arms were folded up in front of him, and his long legs were folded over his arms, and they were held this way by a rubber band.

Raggedy Andy must have wondered why he was being "done up" this way, but it could not have caused him any worry, for in between where his feet came over his face Daddy saw his cheery smile.

After slipping off the rubber band, Daddy smoothed out the wrinkles in Raggedy Andy's arms and legs.

Then Daddy propped Raggedy Ann and Raggedy Andy up against books on his desk so that they sat facing each other, Raggedy Ann's shoe-button eyes looking straight into the shoe-button eyes of Raggedy Andy.

They could not speak—not right out before a real person—so they just sat there and smiled at each other.

Daddy could not help reaching out his hands and feeling their throats.

Yes! There was a lump in Raggedy Ann's throat, and there was a lump in Raggedy Andy's throat. A cotton lump, to be sure, but a lump nevertheless.

"So, Raggedy Ann and Raggedy Andy, that is why you cannot talk, is it?" asked Daddy.

"I will go away and let you have your visit to your-

selves, although it is good to sit and share your happiness by watching you."

Daddy then took the rubber band and placed it around Raggedy Ann's right hand, and around Raggedy Andy's right hand, so that when he had it fixed properly they sat and held each other's hands.

Daddy knew they wished to tell each other all the wonderful things that had happened to them since they had parted more than fifty years before.

So, locking his studio door, Daddy left the two old rag dolls looking into each other's eyes.

The next morning when Daddy unlocked his door and looked at his desk, he saw that Raggedy Andy had fallen over so that he lay with his head in the bend of Raggedy Ann's arm.

The Nursery Dance

When Raggedy Andy was first brought to the nursery he was very quiet. Raggedy Andy did not speak all day, but he smiled pleasantly at all the other dolls. There was Raggedy Ann, the French doll, Henny the little Dutch doll, Uncle Clem, and a few others.

Some of the dolls were without arms and legs.

One had a cracked head. She was a very nice doll, though, and the others all liked her very much. All of them had cried the night Susan (that was her name) fell off the toy box and cracked her china head.

Even though Raggedy Andy did not speak all day, there was really nothing strange about this fact. None of the other dolls spoke all day either. Marcella had played in the nursery all day, and of course they did not speak in front of her.

Marcella thought they did, though, and often had them saying things that they really were not even thinking. For instance, when Marcella served water with sugar in it and little oyster crackers for "tea," Raggedy Andy was thinking of Raggedy Ann, and the French doll was thinking of one time when Fido was lost.

Marcella took the French doll's hand, pressed a cup of tea to Raggedy Andy, and said, "Mr. Raggedy Andy, will you have another cup of tea?" as if the French doll were talking.

And then Marcella answered for Raggedy Andy, "Oh, yes, thank you! It is so delicious!"

Neither the French doll nor Raggedy Andy knew what was going on, for they were thinking real hard to themselves. Nor did they drink the tea when it was poured for them. Marcella drank it instead.

Perhaps this was just as well, for most of the dolls were moist inside from the tea of the day before. Sugar and water, if taken in small quantities, would not give the dolls colic, Marcella would tell them. But she did not know that it made their cotton or sawdust insides quite sticky.

Quite often, too, Marcella forgot to wash their faces after a tea, and Fido would do it for them when he came into the nursery and found the dolls with sweets upon their faces.

Really, Fido was quite a help in this way, but he often missed the corners of their eyes and the backs of their necks where the tea would run and get sticky. But he did his best and saved his little mistress a lot of work.

No, Raggedy Andy did not speak, but he thought a great deal.

One can, you know, when one has been a rag doll as long as Raggedy Andy had. Years and years and years and years! Even Raggedy Ann, with all her wisdom, did not really know how long Raggedy Andy and she had been rag dolls.

If Raggedy Ann had a pencil in her rag hand and Marcella guided it for her, she could count up to ten—sometimes. But why should one worry one's rag head about age when all one's life has been one happy experience after another, with each day filled with love and sunshine?

Raggedy Andy did not know his age, but he remembered many things that had happened years and years and years ago when he and Raggedy Ann were quite young.

It was of these pleasant times Raggedy Andy was thinking all day, and this was the reason he did not notice that Marcella was speaking for him.

Raggedy Andy had to wait patiently for Marcella to put all the dollies to bed and leave them alone in the nursery for the night.

The day might have passed very slowly had it not been for the happy memories that filled Raggedy Andy's cotton-stuffed head.

But he did not even fidget.

Of course he fell out of his chair once, and his shoe-button eyes went *click!* against the floor, but it wasn't his fault. Raggedy Andy was so floppy he could hardly be placed in a chair so that he would stay, especially when Marcella jiggled the table.

Marcella cried, "WAA! WAA!" for Raggedy Andy and picked him up and snuggled him. Then she scolded Uncle Clem for jiggling the table.

Through all this Raggedy Andy kept right on thinking his pleasant thoughts and really did not realize he had fallen from the chair.

You see how easy it is to pass over the little bumps of life if we are happy inside?

And so Raggedy Andy was quiet all day, and the day finally passed.

Raggedy Andy was given one of Uncle Clem's clean

white nighties and shared Uncle Clem's bed. Marcella kissed them all good night and left them to sleep until morning. But as soon as she left the room, all the dolls raised up in their beds. When their little mistress's footsteps passed out of hearing, all the dollies jumped out of their beds and gathered around Raggedy Andy.

Raggedy Ann introduced them one by one, and Raggedy Andy shook hands with each.

"I am very happy to know you all!" he said in a voice as kindly as Raggedy Ann's. "And I hope we will all like each other as much as Raggedy Ann and I have always liked each other!"

"Oh, indeed we shall!" the dollies all answered. "We love Raggedy Ann because she is so kindly and happy, and we know we shall like you, too, for you talk like Raggedy Ann and have the same cheery smile!"

"Now that we know each other so well, what do you say to a game, Uncle Clem?" Raggedy Andy cried as he caught Uncle Clem and danced about the floor.

Henny the Dutch doll dragged the little square music box out into the center of the room and wound it up. Then all, catching hands, danced in a circle around it, laughing and shouting in their tiny doll voices.

"That was lots of fun!" Raggedy Andy said when the music stopped and all the dolls had taken seats upon the floor facing him. "You know I have been shut in a trunk up in an attic for years and years and years."

"Wasn't it very lonesome in the trunk all that time?" Susan asked in her strange little cracked voice.

"Oh, not at all," Raggedy Andy replied, "for there was always a nest of mice down in the corner of the trunk. Cute little mama and daddy mice, and lots of little teeny-weeny baby mice. And when the mama and daddy mice were away, I used to cuddle the tiny little baby mice!"

"No wonder you were never lonesome!" said Uncle Clem, who was very kind and loved everybody and everything.

"No, I was never lonesome in the old trunk in the attic, but it is far more pleasant to be out again and living here with all you nice friends!" said Raggedy Andy.

And all the dolls thought so, too, for already they loved Ragged Andy's happy smile and knew he would prove to be as kindly and lovable as Raggedy Ann.

Raggedy Ann Learns a Lesson

One day the dolls were left all to themselves. Their little mistress had placed them all around the room and told them to be nice children while she was away.

And there they sat and never even so much as wiggled a finger until Marcella had left the room.

Then the tin soldier doll turned his head and solemnly winked at Raggedy Ann. And when the front gate clicked and the dollies knew they were alone in the house, they all scrambled to their feet.

"Now let's have a good time!" cried the tin soldier. "Let's all go in search of something to eat!"

"Yes! Let's all go in search of something to eat!" cried Henny the Dutch doll.

"When Mistress had me out playing with her this morning," said Raggedy Ann, "she carried me by a door near the back of the house, and I smelled something that smelled as if it would taste delicious!"

"Then you lead the way, Raggedy Ann!" cried the French doll.

"I think it would be a good plan to elect Raggedy Ann as our leader on this expedition!" said the tin soldier.

At this all the other dolls clapped their hands together and shouted, "Hurrah! Raggedy Ann will be our leader!"

So Raggedy Ann, very proud indeed to have the confidence and love of all the other dollies, said that she would be very glad to be their leader.

"Follow me!" she cried as her wobbly legs carried her across the floor at a lively pace.

The other dollies followed, racing about the house until they came to the pantry door. "This is the place!" cried Raggedy Ann, and sure enough, all the dollies smelled something that they knew must be very good to eat.

But none of the dollies was tall enough to open the door, and although they pushed and pulled with all their might, the door remained tightly closed.

The dollies were talking and pulling and pushing, and every once in a while one would fall over and the others would step on him or her in their efforts to open the door. Finally Raggedy Ann drew away from the others and sat down on the floor.

When the other dollies discovered Raggedy Ann sitting there running her rag hands through her yarn hair, they knew she was thinking.

"Sh! Sh!" they said to each other and quietly went over near Raggedy Ann and sat down in front of her.

"There must be a way to get inside," said Raggedy Ann.

"Raggedy Ann says there must be a way to get inside!" cried all the dolls.

"I can't seem to think clearly today," Raggedy Ann explained. "It feels as if my head were ripped."

At this the French doll ran to Raggedy Ann and took off her bonnet. "Yes, there is a rip in your head, Raggedy!" she said and pulled a pin from her skirt and pinned up Raggedy's head. "It's not a very neat job, for I got some puckers in it!" she said.

"Oh, that is ever so much better!" cried Raggedy Ann. "Now I can think quite clearly. My thoughts must have leaked out the rip before!"

"Now that I can think so clearly," said Raggedy Ann, "I think the door must be locked, and to get in we must unlock it!"

"That will be easy!" said the Dutch doll who says "Mamma" when he is tipped backward and forward. "For we will have the brave tin soldier shoot the key out of the lock!"

"I can easily do that!" cried the tin soldier as he raised his gun.

"Oh, Raggedy Ann!" cried the French dolly. "Please do not let him shoot!"

"No!" said Raggedy Ann. "We must think of a quieter way!"

After thinking quite hard for a moment Raggedy Ann

jumped up and said, "I have it!" And she caught up the Jumping Jack and held him up to the door; then Jack slid up his stick and unlocked the door.

Then the dollies all pushed, and the door swung open.

My! Such a scramble! The dolls piled over one another in their desire to be the first at the goodies.

They swarmed upon the pantry shelves, and in their eagerness spilled a pitcher of cream, which ran all over the French dolly's dress.

The Dutch doll found some corn bread, and dipping it in the molasses, he sat down for a good feast.

A jar of raspberry jam was overturned, and the dollies ate of this until their faces were all purple.

The tin soldier fell from the shelf three times and bent

one of his tin legs, but he scrambled right back up again.

Never had the dolls had so much fun and excitement, and they had all eaten their fill when they heard the click of the front gate.

They did not take time to climb from the shelves, but all rolled or jumped off to the floor and scrambled back to the nursery as fast as they could run, leaving a trail of bread, crumbs, and jam along the way.

Just as their mistress came into the room the dolls all dropped in whatever positions they happened to be in.

"This is funny!" cried Mistress. "They were all left sitting in their places around the room. I wonder if Fido has been shaking them up." Then she saw Raggedy Ann's face and picked her up. "Why, Raggedy Ann, you are all sticky! I do believe you are covered with jam!" and Mistress tasted Raggedy Ann's hand. "Yes! It *is* jam! Shame on you, Raggedy Ann! You've been in the pantry and all the others, too!" And with this, the dolls' mistress dropped Raggedy Ann on the floor and left the room.

When she came back she had on an apron and her sleeves were rolled up.

She picked up all the sticky dolls, and putting them in a basket, carried them out under the apple tree in the garden.

There she had placed her little tub and wringer, and she took the dolls one at a time and scrubbed them with a scrubbing brush and soused them up and down and this way and that in the soapsuds until they were clean.

Then she hung them all out on the clothesline in the sunshine to dry.

There the dolls hung all day, swinging and twisting about in the breeze.

"I do believe she scrubbed my face so hard that she wore off my smile!" said Raggedy Ann after an hour of silence.

"No, it is still there!" said the tin soldier as the wind twisted him around, so he could see Raggedy. "But I do believe my arms will never work without squeaking. They feel so rusted," he added.

Late in the afternoon the back door opened, and the little mistress came out with a table and chairs. After setting the table she took all the dolls from the line and placed them about the table. They had lemonade with grape jelly in it, which made it a beautiful lavender color, and little "baby-teeny-weeny-cookies" with powdered sugar on them.

After this lovely dinner the dollies were taken in the house, where they had their hair brushed and nice clean nighties put on.

Then they were placed in their beds, and Mistress kissed each one good night and tiptoed from the room.

All the dolls lay as still as mice for a few minutes. Then Raggedy Ann raised up on her cotton-stuffed elbows and said, "I have been thinking our mistress gave us the nice dinner out under the trees to teach us a lesson. She wished us to know that we could have had all the goodies we wished, whenever we wished, if we had behaved ourselves. And our lesson was that we must never take without asking what we could always have for the asking! So let us remember and try never again to do anything that might cause those who love us any unhappiness!"

"Let us all remember," chimed all the other dollies.

And Raggedy Ann, with a merry twinkle in her shoe-button eyes, lay back in her little bed, her cotton head filled with thoughts of love and happiness.

Raggedy Ann and the Painter

When housecleaning time came around, Mistress's mama decided that she would have the nursery repainted and new paper put upon the walls. That was why all the dolls happened to be laid helter-skelter upon one of the high shelves.

Mistress had been in to look at them and wished to put them to bed, but as the painters were coming again early in the morning, Mama thought it best that their beds be piled in the closet.

So the dolls' beds were piled into the closet, one on top of another, and the dolls were placed upon the high shelf.

When all was quiet that night, Raggedy Ann, who was on the bottom of the pile of dolls, spoke softly and asked the others if they would mind moving along the shelf.

"The cotton in my body is getting mashed as flat as a pancake!" said Raggedy Ann. And although the tin soldier was piled so that his foot was pressed into Raggedy's face, she still wore her customary smile.

So the dolls began moving off to one side until Raggedy Ann was free to sit up.

"Ah, that's a great deal better!" she said, stretching her arms and legs to get the kinks out of them and patting her dress into shape.

"Well, I'll be glad when morning comes," she said finally, "for I know Mistress will take us out in the yard and play with us under the trees."

So the dolls sat and talked until daylight, when the painters came to work.

One of the painters, a young fellow, saw the dolls. Reaching up, he took Raggedy Ann down from the shelf.

"Look at this rag doll, Jim," he said to one of the other painters. "She's a daisy." Then he took Raggedy Ann by the hands and danced with her while he whistled a lively tune. Raggedy Ann's heels hit the floor *thumpity-thump,* and she enjoyed it immensely.

The other dolls sat upon the shelf and looked straight before them, for it would never do to let grown-up men know that dolls were really alive.

"Better put her back upon the shelf," said one of the other men. "You'll have the little girl after you! The chances are she likes that old rag doll better than any of the others!"

But the young painter twisted Raggedy Ann into funny attitudes and laughed and laughed as she looped about. Finally he got to tossing her up in the air and catching her. This was great fun for Raggedy, and as she sailed up by the shelf the dolls all smiled at her, for it pleased them whenever Raggedy Ann was happy.

But the young fellow threw Raggedy Ann up into the air once too often, and when she came down he failed to catch her. She came down with a *splash*, headfirst into a bucket of oily paint.

"I told you!" said the older painter. "Now you are in for it!"

"My goodness! I didn't mean to do it!" said the young fellow. "What should I do with her?"

"Better put her back on the shelf!" replied the other.

So Raggedy was placed back upon the shelf, and the paint ran from her head and trickled down upon her dress.

After breakfast Mistress came into the nursery and saw Raggedy all covered with paint, and she began crying.

The young painter felt sorry and told her how it had happened.

"If you will let me," he said, "I will take her home with

me, clean her up tonight, and bring her back the day after tomorrow."

So Raggedy was wrapped in a newspaper that evening and carried away.

All the dolls felt sad that night without Raggedy Ann near them.

"Poor Raggedy! I could have cried when I saw her all covered with paint!" said the French doll.

"She didn't look like our dear old Raggedy Ann at all!" said the tin soldier, who wiped the tears from his eyes so that they would not run down on his arms and rust them.

"The paint covered her lovely smile and nose, and you could not see the laughter in her shoe-button eyes!" said the Dutch doll.

And so the dolls talked that night and the next. But in the daytime when the painters were there, they kept very quiet.

The second day Raggedy was brought home, and the dolls were all anxious for night to come so that they could sit and talk with Raggedy Ann.

At last the painters left and the house was quiet, for Mistress had been in and placed Raggedy on the shelf with the other dolls.

"Tell us all about it, Raggedy dear!" the dolls cried.

"Oh, I am ever so glad I fell in the paint!" cried Raggedy after she had hugged all the dolls. "For I have had the happiest time. The painter took me home and told his mama how I happened to be covered with paint, and

she was very sorry. She took a rag and wiped off my shoe-button eyes, and then I saw that she was a very pretty, sweet-faced lady, and then she got some cleaner and wiped off most of the paint on my face.

"But you know," Raggedy continued, "the paint had soaked through my rag head and had made the cotton inside all sticky and soggy, and I could not think clearly. And my yarn hair was all matted with paint.

"So the kind lady took off my yarn hair and cut the stitches out of my head, and took out all the painty cotton.

"It was a great relief, although it felt queer at first and my thoughts seemed scattered.

"She left me in her workbasket that night and hung me

out upon the clothesline the next morning once she had washed the last of the paint off.

"And while I hung out on the clothesline, what do you think?"

"We could never guess!" all the dolls cried.

"Why, a dear little Jenny Wren came and picked enough cotton out of me to make a cute little cuddly nest in the grape arbor!"

"Wasn't that sweet!" cried all the dolls.

"Yes, indeed it was!" replied Raggedy Ann. "It made me very happy. Then when the lady took me in the house again, she stuffed me with lovely, nice, new cotton all the way from my knees up, sewed me up, and put new yarn on my head for hair and-and-and—it's a secret!" said Raggedy Ann.

"Oh, tell us the secret!" cried all the dolls as they pressed closer to Raggedy Ann.

"Well, I know you will not tell anyone who would not be glad to know about it, so I will tell you the secret and why I am wearing my smile a trifle broader!" said Raggedy Ann.

The dolls all said that Raggedy Ann's smile was indeed a quarter of an inch wider on each side.

"When the dear lady put the new white cotton in my body," said Raggedy Ann, "she went to the cupboard and came back with a paper bag. And she took from the bag ten or fifteen little candy hearts with mottos on them, and she hunted through the candy hearts until she found a beautiful red one, which she sewed up in me with the cotton! So that is the secret, and that is why I am so happy! Feel here," said Raggedy Ann. All the dolls could feel Raggedy Ann's beautiful new candy heart, and they were very happy for her.

After all had hugged each other good night and had cuddled up for the night, the tin soldier asked, "Did you have a chance to see what the motto on your new candy heart is, Raggedy Ann?"

"Oh, yes," replied Raggedy Ann, "I was so happy I forgot to tell you. It has I LOVE YOU printed upon it in nice blue letters."

Doctor Raggedy Andy

Raggedy Andy, Raggedy Ann, Uncle Clem, and Henny were not given medicine because, you see, they had no mouths. That is, mouths through which medicine could be poured. Their mouths were either painted on or sewed on with yarn. Sometimes the medicine spoon would be touched to their faces, but none of the liquid was given to them. Except accidentally

But the French doll had a lovely mouth for taking medicine; it was open and showed her teeth in a dimpling smile. She also had soft blue eyes that opened and closed when she was tilted backward or forward.

The medicine that was given to the dolls had great curing properties. It would cure the most stubborn case of croup, measles, whooping cough, or any other ailment the dolls' little mistress wished upon them.

Some days all the dolls would be put to bed with "measles," but in the course of half an hour they would have every other ailment in the doctor book.

The dolls enjoyed it very much, for you see, Marcella always tried the medicine first to see if it was strong enough before she gave any to the dolls. So really the dolls did not get as much of the medicine as their little mistress.

The wonderful remedy was made from a very old recipe handed down from ancient times.

This recipe is guaranteed to cure every ill a doll may have.

The medicine was made from brown sugar and water.

Perhaps you may have used it for your dollies.

The medicine was also used as "tea" and "soda water," except when the dolls were supposed to be ill.

Having nothing but painted or yarn mouths, the ailments of Raggedy Andy, Raggedy Ann, Uncle Clem, and Henny the Dutch doll mostly consisted of sprained wrists, arms, and legs, or perhaps a headache and a toothache.

None of them knew they had the trouble until Marcella had wrapped up the "injured" rag arm, leg, or head, and had explained in detail just what was the matter.

Raggedy Andy, Raggedy Ann, Uncle Clem, and Henny were just as happy with their heads tied up for the toothache as they were without their heads tied up.

Not having teeth, naturally they could not have the toothache, but if they could furnish amusement for Marcella by having her pretend they had the toothache, then that made them very happy.

So this day the French doll was quite ill. She started out with the "croup," and went through the "measles," "whooping cough," and "yellow fever" in an hour.

The attack came on quite suddenly.

The French doll was sitting quietly in one of the little red chairs, smiling the prettiest of dimpling smiles at Raggedy Andy and thinking of the romp the dolls would have that night after the house grew quiet, when Marcella discovered that the French doll had the "croup" and put her to bed.

The French doll closed her eyes when put to bed, but the rest of her face did not change expression. She still wore her happy smile.

Marcella mixed the medicine very "strong" and poured it into the French doll's open mouth. She was given a dose every minute or so.

It was during the "yellow fever" stage that Marcella was called in to supper and left the dolls in the nursery alone.

Marcella did not play with them again that evening, so the dolls all remained in the same position until Marcella and the rest of the folks went to bed.

Then Raggedy Andy jumped from his chair and wound up the little music box. "Let's start with a lively dance!" he cried.

When the music started tinkling he caught the French doll's hand and danced across the nursery floor before he discovered that her soft blue eyes remained closed as they were when she lay upon the "sick" bed.

All the dolls gathered around Raggedy Andy and the French doll.

JOHNNY GRUELLE.

"I can't open my eyes!" she said.

Raggedy Andy tried to open the French doll's eyes with his soft rag hands, but it was no use. They shook her again and again. It was no use; her eyes remained closed.

"It must be the sticky, sugary medicine!" said Uncle Clem.

"I really believe it must be!" the French doll replied. "The medicine seemed to settle in the back of my head when I was lying down, and I can still feel it back there!"

"That must be it, and now it has hardened and keeps your pretty eyes from working!" said Raggedy Ann. "What shall we do?"

Raggedy Andy and Raggedy Ann walked over to a corner of the nursery and thought and thought. They pulled their foreheads down into wrinkles with their hands so that they might think harder.

Finally Raggedy Ann cried, "I've thought of a plan!" and went skipping from the corner out to where the other dolls sat about the French doll.

"We must stand her upon her head so that the medicine will run up into her hair, for there is a hole in the top of her head. I remember seeing it when her hair came off one time!"

"No sooner said than done!" cried Uncle Clem as he took the French doll by the waist and stood her upon her head.

"That should be long enough!" Raggedy Ann said when Uncle Clem had held the French doll in this position for five minuets.

But when the French doll was again placed upon her feet, her eyes still remained tightly closed.

All this time Raggedy Andy had remained in the corner, thinking as hard as his rag head would think.

He thought and thought until the yarn hair upon his head stood up in the air and wiggled.

"If the medicine did not run up into her hair when she stood upon her head," thought Raggedy Andy, "then it is because the medicine could not run; so, if the medicine cannot run, it is because it is too sticky and thick to run out the hole in the top of her head."

He also thought a lot more. At last he turned to the others and said out loud, "I can't seem to think of a single way to help her open her eyes unless we take off her hair and wash the medicine from inside her china head."

"Why didn't I think of that?" Raggedy Ann asked.

"That is just the way we shall have to do it!"

So Raggedy Ann caught hold of the French doll's feet, and Raggedy Andy caught hold of the French doll's lively curls, and they pulled and they pulled.

Then the other dolls caught hold of Raggedy Ann and Raggedy Andy and pulled and pulled, until finally, with a sharp *R—R—Rip!* the French doll's hair came off, and the dolls who were pulling went tumbling over backward.

Laughingly, they scrambled to their feet and sat the French doll up, so they might look into the hole in the top of her head.

Yes, the sticky medicine had grown hard and would not let the French doll's eyes open.

Raggedy Andy put his hand inside and pushed on the eyes so that they opened.

This was all right, only now the eyes would not close when the French doll lay down. She tried it.

So Raggedy Andy ran down into the kitchen and brought up a small tin cup full of warm water and a tiny rag.

With these he loosened the sticky medicine and washed the inside of the French doll's head nice and clean. (There were lots of cookie and cracker crumbs inside her head too.)

Raggedy Andy washed it all nice and clean, and then wet the glue, which made the pretty curls stay on.

So when her hair was placed upon her head again, the French doll was as good as new.

"Thank you all very much!" she said as she tilted backward

and forward and found that her eyes worked very easily.

Raggedy Andy again wound up the little music box, and catching the French doll about the waist, started a rollicking dance that lasted until the roosters in the neighborhood began their morning crowing.

Then, knowing the folks might soon be awake, the dolls left their playing, and all took the same positions they had been in when Marcella left them the night before.

And so Marcella found them.

The French doll was in bed with her eyes closed and her happy dimpling smile lighting up her pretty face.

And to this day the dollies' little mistress does not know that Raggedy Andy was the doctor who cured the French doll of her only ill.

Raggedy Ann's Trip on the River

When Marcella had a tea party out in the orchard, of course all of the dolls were invited. Raggedy Ann, the tin soldier, the Indian doll, and all the others—even the four little penny dolls in the spool box. After a lovely tea party with ginger cookies and milk, of course the dolls were very sleepy. At least Marcella thought they were, so she took all except Raggedy Ann into the house and put them to bed for their afternoon nap. Marcella had told Raggedy Ann to stay there and watch the things.

As there was nothing else to do, Raggedy Ann waited for Marcella to return. And as she watched the little ants eating the cookie crumbs Marcella had thrown to them, she suddenly heard the patter of puppy feet behind her. It was Fido.

The puppy dog ran up to Raggedy Ann and tilted his head as he looked at her. Then he put his front feet out and barked in Raggedy Ann's face. Raggedy Ann tried to look very stern, but she could not hide the broad smile painted on her face.

"Oh, you want to play, do you?" the puppy dog barked as he jumped at Raggedy Ann and then jumped back again.

The more Raggedy Ann smiled, the livelier Fido's antics became until finally he caught the end of her dress and dragged her about.

This was great fun for the puppy dog, but Raggedy Ann did not enjoy it. She kicked and twisted as much as she could, but the puppy dog thought Raggedy Ann was playing.

He ran out the garden gate and down the path across the meadow, every once in a while stopping and pretending he was very angry. When he pretended this, Fido would give Raggedy Ann a great shaking, making her yarn head hit the ground *ratty-tat-tat*. Then he would give his head a toss and send Raggedy Ann high in the air where she would turn over two or three times before she reached the ground.

By this time she had lost her apron, and some of her yarn hair was coming loose.

As Fido neared the brook another puppy dog came running across the footbridge to meet him. "What have you there, Fido?" said the new puppy as he bounced up to the rag doll.

"This is Raggedy Ann," answered Fido. "She and I are having a lovely time playing."

You see, Fido really thought Raggedy enjoyed being tossed and whirled high up in the air. But she didn't. However the game didn't last much longer. As Raggedy Ann hit the ground the new puppy dog caught her dress and ran with her across the bridge, Fido barking close behind him.

In the center of the bridge Fido caught up with the new puppy dog and they had a lively tug-of-war with Raggedy Ann stretched between them. As they pulled and tugged and flopped Raggedy Ann about, somehow she fell over the side of the bridge into the water.

The puppy dogs were surprised, and Fido was very sorry indeed, for he remembered how good Raggedy Ann had been to him and how she had rescued him from the dog pound. But the current carried Raggedy Ann right along, and all Fido could do was run along the bank and bark.

Now you would have thought Raggedy Ann would sink, but no, she floated nicely, for she was stuffed with clean white cotton, and the water didn't soak through very quickly.

After a while the strange puppy and Fido grew tired of running along the bank, and the strange puppy scampered home over the meadow with his tail carried gaily over his back as if he had done nothing to be ashamed of. But Fido walked home very sorry indeed. His little heart was broken to think that he had caused Raggedy Ann to be drowned.

But Raggedy Ann didn't drown. No, not at all. In fact she even went to sleep on the brook, for the motion of the current was very soothing as it carried her along. It was just like being rocked by Marcella.

So, sleeping peacefully, Raggedy Ann drifted along with the current until she came to a pool where she lodged against a large stone.

Raggedy Ann tried to climb up on the stone, but she was so heavy from the water she could not climb.

So there she had to stay until Marcella and Daddy came along and found her.

You see, they had been looking for her. They had found pieces of her apron all along the path and across the meadow where Fido and the strange puppy dog had shaken them from Raggedy Ann. So they followed the

brook until they found her floating on her back.

Marcella hurried home and took off all of Raggedy Ann's wet clothes and placed her on a little red chair in front of the oven door, and then she brought all of the other dolls in and read a fairy tale to them while Raggedy Ann steamed and dried.

When Raggedy Ann was thoroughly dry, Mama said she thought the cake must be finished, and she took from the oven a lovely chocolate cake and gave Marcella a large piece to have another tea party with.

That night when all the house was asleep, Raggedy Ann rose up in bed and said to the dolls who were still awake, "I am so happy that I do not feel a bit sleepy. Do you know, I believe the water soaked me so thoroughly my candy heart must have melted and filled my whole body, for I do not feel the least bit angry with Fido for playing with me so roughly!"

The Taffy Pull

"I know how we can have a whole lot of fun!" Raggedy Andy said to the other dolls. "Let's have a taffy pull.

"Do you mean crack-the-whip, Raggedy Andy?" asked the French doll.

"He means a tug-of-war, don't you, Raggedy Andy?" asked Henny.

"No," Raggedy Andy replied, "I mean a taffy pull!"

"If it's lots of fun, then show us how to play the game!" Uncle Clem said. "We like to have fun, don't we?" And Uncle Clem turned to all the other dolls as he asked the question.

"It really is not a game," Raggedy Andy explained. "You see, it is only a taffy pull."

"We take sugar and water and butter and a little vinegar and put it all on the stove to cook. When it has cooked until it strings way out when you dip some up in a spoon or gets hard when you drop some of it in a cup of water, then it is candy.

"Then it must be placed upon buttered plates until it has cooled a little, and then each one takes some of the candy and pulls and pulls until it gets real white. Then it is called 'Taffy.'"

"That will be loads of fun!" "Show us how to begin!" "Let's have a taffy pull!" "Come on, everybody!" the dolls cried.

"Just one moment!" Raggedy Ann said. She had remained quiet before, for she had been thinking very hard, so hard, in fact, that two stitches had burst in the

back of her rag head. The dolls, in their eagerness to have the taffy pull, were dancing about Raggedy Andy, but when Raggedy Ann spoke in her soft cottony voice, they all quieted down and waited for her to speak again.

"I was just thinking," Raggedy Ann said, "that it would be very nice to have the taffy pull, but suppose some of the folks smell the candy while it is cooking!"

"There is no one at home!" Raggedy Andy said. "I thought of that, Raggedy Ann. They have all gone over to Cousin Jenny's house and will not be back until the day after tomorrow. I heard Mama tell Marcella."

"If that is the case, we can have the taffy pull and all the fun that goes with it!" Raggedy Ann cried as she started for the nursery door.

After her ran all the dollies, their little feet pitter-patting across the floor and down the hall.

When they came to the stairway, Raggedy Ann, Raggedy Andy, Uncle Clem, and Henny threw themselves down the stairs, turning over and over as they fell.

The other dolls, having china heads, had to be much more careful, so they slid down the banisters or jumped from one stop to another.

Raggedy Ann, Raggedy Andy, Uncle Clem, and Henny piled in a heap at the bottom of the steps, and by the time they had untangled themselves and helped each other up, the other dolls were down the stairs.

To the kitchen they all raced. There they found the fire in the stove still burning.

Raggedy Andy brought a small stew kettle while the others brought the sugar, vinegar, and water, and a large spoon.

Raggedy Andy stood upon the stove and watched the candy, dipping into it every once in a while to see if it had cooked long enough, and stirring it with the large spoon.

At last the candy began to string out from the spoon when it was held above the stew kettle, and after trying a few drops in a cup of cold water, Raggedy Andy pronounced it "done."

Uncle Clem pulled out a large platter from the pantry, and Raggedy Ann dipped her rag hand into the butter jar and buttered the platter.

The candy, when it was poured into the platter, was a lovely golden color and smelled delicious to the dolls.

Henny could not wait until it cooled, so he put one of his chamois skin hands into the hot candy.

Of course it did not burn Henny, but when he pulled his hand out again, it was covered with a great ball of candy, which strung out all over the kitchen floor and got upon his clothes.

Then, too, the candy cooled quickly, and in a very short time Henny's hand was encased in a hard ball of candy. Henny couldn't wiggle any of his fingers on that hand, and he was sorry he had been so hasty.

While waiting for the candy to cool, Raggedy Andy said, "We must rub butter upon our hands before we pull the candy, or otherwise it will stick to our hands as it has done to Henny's hands and will have to wear off!"

"Will this hard ball of candy have to wear off of my hand?" Henny asked. "It is so hard, I cannot wiggle any of my fingers!"

"It will either have to wear off or you will have to soak your hand in water for a long time until the candy on it melts!" said Raggedy Andy.

"Dear me!" said Henny.

Uncle Clem brought the poker then, and asking Henny to put his hand upon the stove leg, he gave the hard candy a few sharp taps with the poker and chipped the candy from Henny's hand.

"Thank you, Uncle Clem!" Henny said as he wiggled his fingers. "That feels much better!"

Raggedy Andy told all the dolls to rub butter upon their hands.

"The candy is getting cool enough to pull!" he said.

Then, when all the dolls had their hands nice and buttery, Raggedy Andy cut them each a nice piece of candy and showed them how to pull it.

"Take it in one hand this way," he said, "and pull it with the other hand, like this!"

When all the dolls were supplied with candy they sat

about and pulled it, watching it grow whiter and more sil–very the longer they pulled.

Then, when the taffy was real white, it began to grow harder, and harder, so the smaller dolls could scarcely pull it anymore.

When this happened, Raggedy Andy, Raggedy Ann, Uncle Clem, and Henny, who were larger, took the little dolls' candy and mixed it with what they had been pulling until all the taffy was snow white.

Then Raggedy Andy pulled it out into a long rope and held it while Uncle Clem gave the ends a sharp tap with the edge of the spoon.

This snipped the taffy into small pieces, just as easily as you might break icicles with a few sharp taps of a stick.

The small pieces of white taffy were placed upon the buttered platter again, and the dolls all danced about it,

singing and laughing, for this had been the most fun they had had for a long, long time.

"But what shall we do with it?" Raggedy Ann asked.

"Yes, what shall we do with it!" Uncle Clem said. "We can't let it remain in the platter here upon the kitchen floor! We must hide it, or do something with it!"

"While we are trying to think of a way to dispose of it, let us wash the stew kettle and the spoon!" said practical Raggedy Ann.

"That is a very happy thought, Raggedy Ann!" said Raggedy Andy. "For it will clean the butter and candy from our hands while we are doing it!"

So the stew kettle was dragged to the sink and filled with water, and the dolls all took turns scraping the candy from the sides of the kettle and scrubbing the inside with a cloth.

When the kettle was nice and clean and had been wiped dry, Raggedy Andy found a roll of waxed paper in the pantry upon one of the shelves.

"We'll wrap each piece of taffy in a nice little piece of paper," he said. "Then we'll find a nice paper bag, and put all the pieces inside the bag, and throw it from the upstairs window when someone passes the house so that someone may have the candy!"

All the dolls gathered about the platter on the floor, and while Raggedy Andy cut the paper into neat squares, the dolls wrapped the taffy in the papers.

Then the taffy was put into a large bag, and with much pulling and tugging it was finally dragged up into the

nursery, where a window faced out toward the street.

Then just as a little boy and a little girl, who looked as though they did not ever have much candy, passed the house, the dolls all gave the bag a push and sent it tumbling to the sidewalk.

The two children laughed and shouted, "Thank you!" when they saw that the bag contained candy, and the dolls, peeping from behind the lace curtains, watched the two happy-faced children eating the taffy as they skipped down the street.

When the children had passed out of sight the dolls climbed down from the window.

"That was lots of fun!" said the French doll as she smoothed her skirts and sat down beside Raggedy Andy.

"Oh, I almost forgot to tell you," said Raggedy Andy, "that when pieces of taffy are wrapped in little pieces of paper, just as we wrapped them, they are called 'kisses.'"

"How lovely! I believe Raggedy Andy must have a candy heart, too, like Raggedy Ann!" said Uncle Clem.

"No!" Raggedy Andy answered. "I'm just stuffed with white cotton, and I have no candy heart, but someday perhaps I shall have!"

"A candy heart is very nice!" Raggedy Ann said. (You know, she had one.) "But one can be just as nice and happy and full of sunshine without a candy heart."

Raggedy Ann and the Strange Dolls

Raggedy Ann lay just as Marcella had dropped her — all sprawled out with her rag arms and legs twisted in ungraceful attitudes. Her yarn hair was twisted and lay partly over her face, hiding one of her shoe-button eyes.

"Did you ever see such an ungainly creature!"

"I do believe it has shoe buttons for eyes!"

"And yarn hair!"

"Mercy, did you ever see such feet!"

Raggedy gave no sign that she had heard, but lay there smiling at the ceiling. Perhaps Raggedy Ann knew that what the new dolls said was true. But sometimes the truth may hurt, and this may have been the reason Raggedy Ann lay there so still.

The Dutch doll rolled off the doll sofa and said "Mamma" in his quivery voice; he was so surprised at hearing anyone speak so horribly of beloved Raggedy Ann—dear Raggedy Ann, whom all the dolls loved.

Uncle Clem was also very much surprised and offended. He walked up in front of the two new dolls and looked them sternly in the eyes, but he could think of nothing to say, so he pulled at his yarn mustache.

Marcella had only received the two new dolls that morning. They had come in the morning mail and were presents from an aunt.

Marcella had named the two new dolls Annabel-Lee and Thomas after her aunt and uncle.

Annabel-Lee and Thomas were beautiful dolls and

must have cost heaps and heaps of shiny pennies, for both were very handsomely dressed and had *real* hair!

Annabel-Lee's hair was a lovely shade of auburn, and Thomas's was golden yellow.

Annabel-Lee was dressed in a soft, lace-covered silk gown, and upon her head she wore a beautiful hat with long silk ribbons tied in a neat bowknot beneath her dimpled chin.

Thomas was dressed in an Oliver Twist suit of dark velvet with a lace collar. Both he and Annabel-Lee wore lovely black slippers and short stockings.

They were sitting upon two of the little red doll chairs, where Marcella had placed them and where they could see the other dolls.

When Uncle Clem walked in front of them and pulled his mustache, they laughed outright. "Tee-hee-hee!" they

snickered. "He has holes in his knees!"

Quite true. Uncle Clem was made of worsted, and the moths had eaten his knees and part of his kiltie. He had a kiltie, you see, for Uncle Clem was a Scotch doll.

Uncle Clem shook, but he felt so hurt he could think of nothing to say.

He walked over and sat down beside Raggedy Ann and brushed her yarn hair away from her shoe-button eye.

The tin soldier went over and sat beside them.

"Don't you mind what they say, Raggedy!" he said. "They do not know you as we do!"

"We don't care to know her!" said Annabel-Lee as she primped her dress. "She looks like a scarecrow!"

"And that soldier must have been made with a can opener!" laughed Thomas.

"You should be ashamed of yourselves!" said the French dolly as she stood before Annabel-Lee and Thomas. "You will make all of us sorry that you have joined our family if you continue to poke fun and look down upon us. We are all happy here together and share in each other's adventures and happiness."

Now, that night Marcella did not undress the two new dolls, for she had no nighties for them, so she let them sit up in the two little red doll chairs, so they would not muss their clothes. "I will make nighties for you tomorrow!" she said as she kissed them good night. Then she went over and gave Raggedy Ann a good-night hug. "Take good care of all my children, Raggedy!" she said as she went out.

Annabel-Lee and Thomas whispered together. "Perhaps we have been too hasty in our judgment!" said Annabel-Lee. "This Raggedy Ann seems to be a favorite with the mistress and with all the dolls!"

"There must be a reason!" replied Thomas. "I am beginning to feel sorry that we spoke of her looks. One really cannot help one's looks after all."

Now, Annabel-Lee and Thomas were very tired after their long journey, and soon they fell asleep and forgot all about the other dolls.

When they were sound asleep Raggedy Ann slipped quietly from her bed and awakened the tin soldier and Uncle Clem, and the three tiptoed to the two beautiful new dolls.

They lifted them gently so as not to awaken them and carried them carefully to Raggedy Ann's bed.

Raggedy Ann tucked them in snugly and lay down upon the hard floor.

The tin soldier and Uncle Clem both tried to coax Raggedy Ann into accepting their bed (they slept together), but Raggedy Ann would not hear of it.

"I am stuffed with nice soft cotton, and the hard floor does not bother me at all!" said Raggedy.

At daybreak the next morning Annabel-Lee and Thomas awakened to find themselves in Raggedy Ann's bed. As they rose up and looked at each other, each knew how ashamed the other felt, for they knew Raggedy Ann had generously given them her bed.

There Raggedy Ann lay, all sprawled out upon the hard floor, her rag arms and legs twisted in ungraceful attitudes.

"How good and honest she looks!" said Annabel-Lee. "It must be her shoe-button eyes!"

"How nicely her yarn hair falls in loops over her face!" exclaimed Thomas. "I did not notice how pleasant her face looked last night!"

"The others seem to love her ever and ever so much!" mused Annabel. "It must be because she is so kind."

Both new dolls were silent for a while, thinking deeply.

"How do you feel?" Thomas finally asked.

"Very much ashamed of myself!" answered Annabel-Lee. "And you, Thomas?"

"As soon as Raggedy Ann awakens, I shall tell her how

ashamed I am of myself, and if she can, I want her to for-give me!" Thomas said.

"The more I look at her, the better I like her!" said Annabel-Lee.

"I am going to kiss her!" said Thomas.

"You'll awaken her if you do!" said Annabel-Lee.

But Thomas climbed out of bed and kissed Raggedy Ann on her painted cheek and smoothed her yarn hair from her rag forehead.

And Annabel-Lee climbed out of bed, too, and kissed Raggedy Ann.

Then Thomas and Annabel-Lee gently carried Raggedy Ann and put her in her own bed and tenderly tucked her in, and then took their seats in the two little red chairs.

After a while Annabel-Lee said softly to Thomas, "I feel ever and ever so much better and happier!"

"So do I!" Thomas replied. "It's like a whole lot of sunshine coming into a dark room, and I shall always try to keep it there!"

Fido had one fuzzy white ear sticking up over the edge of his basket, and he gave his tail a few thumps against his pillow.

Raggedy Ann lay quietly in bed where Thomas and Annabel had tucked her. And as she smiled at the ceiling her candy heart (with I LOVE YOU written on it) thrilled with contentment, for as you have probably guessed, Raggedy Ann had not been asleep at all!

Raggedy Ann's New Sisters

Marcella was having a tea party up in the nursery when Daddy called to her, so she left the dollies sitting around the tiny table and ran downstairs carrying Raggedy Ann with her.

Mama, Daddy, and a strange man were talking in the living room, and Daddy introduced Marcella to the stranger.

The stranger was a large man with kindly eyes and a cheery smile, as pleasant as Raggedy Ann's.

He took Marcella upon his knee and ran his fingers through her curls as he talked to Daddy and Mama, so of course, Raggedy Ann liked him from the beginning. "I have two little girls," he told Marcella. "Their names are Virginia and Doris, and one time when we were at the seashore, they were playing in the sand and they covered up Freddy, Doris's boy doll, in the sand. They were playing that Freddy was bathing and that he wanted to be covered with the clean white sand, just as the other bathers did. And when they had covered Freddy they took their little pails and shovels and went farther down the beach to play and forgot all about him.

"Now, when it came time for us to go home, Virginia and Doris remembered Freddy and ran down to get him. But the tide had come in and Freddy was way out under the water, and they could not find him. Virginia and Doris were very sad, and they talked of Freddy the whole way home."

"It was too bad they forgot Freddy," said Marcella.

"Yes, indeed it was!" the new friend replied as he took Raggedy Ann up and made her dance on Marcella's knee. "But it turned out all right after all, for do you know what happened to Freddy?"

"No, what did happen to him?" Marcella asked.

"Well, first of all, when Freddy was covered with the sand, he enjoyed it immensely. And he did not mind it so much when the tide came up over him, for he believed that Virginia and Doris would return and get him.

"But soon Freddy felt the sand above him move as if someone was digging him out. Then his head was uncovered, and he could look right up through the pretty green water, and what do you think was happening? The Tide Fairies were uncovering Freddy!

"When he was completely uncovered, the Tide Fairies swam with Freddy way out to the Undertow Fairies. The Undertow Fairies took Freddy and swam with him way out and eventually carried Freddy up to the surface and tossed him up to the Spray Fairies, who carried him to the Wind Fairies."

"And the Wind Fairies?" Marcella asked breathlessly.

"The Wind Fairies carried Freddy right to our garden, and there Virginia and Doris found him, none the worse for his wonderful adventure!"

"Freddy must have enjoyed it, and your little girls must have been very glad to get Freddy back again!" said Marcella. "Raggedy Ann went up in the air on the tail of a kite one day and fell and was lost, so now I am very careful with her!"

"Would you let me take Raggedy Ann for a few days?" asked the new friend.

Marcella was silent. She liked the stranger friend, but she did not wish to lose Raggedy Ann.

"I will promise to take very good care of her and return her to you in a week. Will you let her go with me, Marcella?"

Marcella finally agreed and when the stranger friend left, he placed Raggedy Ann in his bag.

"It is lonely without Raggedy Ann!" said the dollies each night.

"We miss her happy painted smile and her cheery ways!" they said.

And so the week dragged by . . .

But, my! What chatter there was in the nursery the first night after Raggedy Ann returned. All the dolls were so anxious to hug Raggedy Ann that they could scarcely wait until Marcella had left them alone.

When they had squeezed Raggedy Ann almost out of

shape, and she had smoothed out her yarn hair, patted her apron out, and felt her shoe-button eyes to see if they were still there, she said, "Well, what have you been doing? Tell me all the news!"

"Oh, we have just had the usual tea parties and games!" said the tin soldier. "Tell us about yourself, Raggedy dear. We have missed you so much!"

"Yes! Tell us where you have been and what you have done, Raggedy!" all the dolls cried.

But Raggedy Ann just then noticed that one of the penny dolls had a hand missing.

"How did this happen?" she asked as she picked up the doll.

"I fell off the table and fell upon the tin soldier last night when we were playing. But don't mind a little thing like that, Raggedy Ann," replied the penny doll. "Tell us of yourself! Have you had a nice time?"

"I shall not tell a thing until your hand is mended!" Raggedy Ann said.

So the Indian doll ran and brought a bottle of glue. "Where's the hand?" Raggedy asked.

"In my pocket," the penny doll answered.

When Raggedy Ann had glued the penny doll's hand in place and wrapped a rag around it to hold it until the glue dried, she said, "When I tell you of this wonderful adventure, I know you will all feel very happy. It has made me almost burst my stitches with joy."

The dolls all sat upon the floor around Raggedy Ann, the tin soldier with his arm over her shoulder.

"Well, first when I left," said Raggedy Ann, "I was placed in the Stranger Friend's bag. It was rather stuffy in there, but I did not mind it; in fact I believe that I fell asleep, for when I awakened I saw the Stranger Friend's hand reaching into the bag. Then he lifted me out and danced me upon his knee. 'What do you think of her?' he asked to three other men sitting nearby.

"I was so interested in looking out of the window, I did not pay any attention to what they said, for we were on a train and the scenery was just flying by! Then I was put back in the bag.

"When next I was taken out, I was in a large, clean, light room, and there were many, many girls all dressed in white aprons.

"The Stranger Friend showed me to another man and to the girls who took off my clothes, cut my seams, and took out my cotton. And what do you think! They found my lovely candy heart had not melted at all as I thought. Then they laid me on a table and marked all around my outside edges with a pencil on clean white cloth, and then the girls restuffed me and dressed me.

"I stayed in the clean, big, light room for two or three days and nights and watched my Sisters grow from pieces of cloth into rag dolls just like myself!"

"Your SISTERS!" the dolls all exclaimed in astonishment. "What do you mean, Raggedy?"

"I mean," said Raggedy Ann, "that the Stranger Friend had borrowed me from Marcella so that he could have patterns made from me. And before I left the big, clean,

white room, there were hundreds of rag dolls so like me you would not have been able to tell us apart."

"We could have told *you* by your happy smile!" cried the French dolly.

"But all of my Sister dolls have smiles just like mine!" replied Raggedy Ann.

"And shoe-button eyes?" the dolls all asked.

"Yes, shoe-button eyes!" Raggedy Ann replied.

"I would tell you from the others by your dress, Raggedy Ann," said the French doll. "Your dress is fifty years old! I could tell you by that!"

"But my new Sister rag dolls have dresses just like mine, for the Stranger Friend had cloth made especially for them exactly like mine."

"I know how we could tell you from the other rag dolls, even if you all look exactly alike!" said the Indian doll, who had been thinking for a long time.

"How?" asked Raggedy Ann with a laugh.

"By feeling your candy heart! If the doll has a candy heart, then it is you, Raggedy Ann!"

Raggedy Ann laughed, "I am so glad you all love me as you do, but I am sure you would not be able to tell me from my new Sisters except that I am more worn. For each new rag doll has a candy heart, and on it is written, I LOVE YOU, just as is written on my own candy heart."

"And there are hundreds and hundreds of the new rag dolls?" asked the little penny dolls.

"Hundreds and hundreds of them, all named Raggedy Ann," replied Raggedy.

"Then," said the penny dolls, "we are indeed happy and proud for you! For wherever one of the new Raggedy Ann dolls goes, there will go with it all the love and happiness that *you* give to others."

The Singing Shell

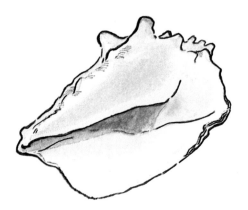

For years and years the beautiful shell had been upon the floor in Grandma's front room. It was a large shell with many points upon it. These were coarse and rough, but the shell was most beautiful inside.

Marcella had seen the shell time and time again and often admired its lovely coloring, which could be seen when one looked inside the shell.

So one day Grandma gave the beautiful shell to Marcella to have for her very own, up in the nursery.

"It will be nice to place before the nursery door, so the wind will not blow the door shut and pinch anyone's fingers!" Grandma said.

So Marcella brought the shell home and placed it in front of the nursery door. Here the dolls saw it that night when all of the house was still, and stood about it wondering what kind of toy it might be.

"It seems to be nearly all mouth!" said Henny the Dutch doll. "Perhaps it can talk."

"It has teeth!" the French doll pointed out. "It may bite!"

"I do not believe it will bite," Raggedy Andy mused as he got down upon his hands and knees and looked up into the shell. "Marcella would not have it up here if it would bite!" And saying this, Raggedy Andy put his rag arm into the lovely shell's mouth.

"It doesn't bite! I knew it wouldn't!" he cried. "Just feel how smooth it is inside!"

All the dolls felt and were surprised to find it polished

so highly inside, while the outside was so coarse and rough. With the help of Uncle Clem and Henny, Raggedy Andy turned the shell upon its back so that all the dolls might look in.

The coloring consisted of dainty pinks, creamy whites, and pale blues all running together, just as the coloring in an opal runs from one shade into another. Raggedy Andy, stooping over to look farther up inside the pretty shell, heard something.

"It's whispering!" he said as he raised up in surprise.

All the dolls took turns putting their ears to the mouth of the beautiful shell. Yes, truly it whispered, but they could not catch just what it said.

Finally Raggedy Andy suggested that all the dolls lie down upon the floor directly before the shell and keep very quiet.

"If we don't make a sound, we may be able to hear what it says!" he explained.

So the dolls lay down, placing themselves flat upon the

floor directly in front of the shell and where they could see and admire its beautiful coloring.

Now, the dolls could be very, very quiet when they really wished to be, and it was easy for them to hear the faint whispering of the shell.

This is the story the shell told the dolls in the nursery that night:

"A long, long time ago, I lived upon the yellow sand, deep down beneath the blue, blue waters of the ocean. Pretty silken seaweeds grew around my home and reached their waving branches up, up toward the top of the water.

"Through the pretty seaweeds, fishes of pretty colors and shapes darted here and there, playing at their games.

"It was still and quiet way down where I lived, for even if the ocean roared and pounded itself into an angry mass of tumbling waves up above, this never disturbed the calm waters down where I lived.

"Many times little fishes or other tiny sea people came and hid within my pretty house when they were being pursued by larger sea creatures. And it always made me very happy to give them this protection.

"They would stay inside until I whispered that the larger creature had gone. Then they would leave me and return to their play.

"Pretty little sea horses with slender, curving bodies often went sailing above me or would come to rest upon my back. It was nice to lie and watch the tiny things curl their little tails about the seaweed and talk together, for the sea horses like one another and are gentle and kind to

each other, sharing their food happily and smoothing their little ones with their cunning noses.

"But one day a diver leaped over the side of a boat and came swimming headfirst down, down to where I lay. My! How the tiny sea creatures scurried to hide from him. He took me within his hand, and giving his feet a thump upon the yellow sand, rose with me to the surface.

"He poured the water from me, and out came all the little creatures who had been hiding there!"

Raggedy Andy wiggled upon the floor; he was so interested.

"Did the tiny creatures get back into the water safely?" he asked the beautiful shell.

"Oh, yes!" the shell whispered in reply. "The man held me over the side of the boat, so the tiny creatures went safely back into the water!"

"I am so glad!" Raggedy Andy said with a sigh of relief. "He must have been a kindly man!"

"Yes, indeed!" the beautiful shell replied. "So I was placed along with a lot of other shells in the bottom of the boat, and every once in a while another shell was placed among us. We whispered together and wondered where we were going. We were finally sold to different people, and I have been at Grandma's house for a long, long time."

"You lived there when Grandma was a little girl, didn't you?" Raggedy Ann asked.

"Yes," replied the shell. "I have lived there ever since Grandma was a little girl. She often used to play with me and listen to me sing."

"Raggedy Ann can play 'Peter, Peter, Pumpkin Eater' on the piano with one hand," said Uncle Clem. "But none of us can sing. Will you sing for us?" he asked the shell.

"I sing all the time," the shell replied, "for I cannot help singing. But my singing is a secret, so it is very soft and low. Put your head close to the opening in my shell and listen!"

The dolls took turns doing this, and heard the shell sing softly and very sweetly.

"It is queer that anything so rough on the outside could be so pretty within!" said Raggedy Andy. "It must be a great pleasure to be able to sing so sweetly!"

"Indeed it is," replied the beautiful shell, "and I get a great happiness from singing all the time."

"And you will bring lots of pleasure to us by being so happy!" said Raggedy Andy. "For although you may not enter into our games, we will always know that you are happily singing, and that will make us all happy!"

"I will tell you the secret of my singing," said the shell. "When anyone puts his ear to me and listens, he hears the reflection of his own heart's music; so, you see, while I say that I am singing all the time, in reality I sing only when someone full of happiness hears his own singing as if it were mine."

"How unselfish you are to say this!" said Raggedy Andy. "Now we are ever so much more glad to have you with us. Aren't we?" he asked, turning to the rest of the dolls.

"Yes, indeed!" came the answer from all the dolls, even the tiny penny dolls.

"That is why the shell is so beautiful inside!" said Raggedy Ann. "Those who are unselfish may wear rough clothes, but inside they are always beautiful, just like the shell, and reflect to others the happiness and sunny music within their hearts!"